King of Dilly Dally

BEST OF LUCK!

Written by Michael D. Scott

Illustrations by Megan D. Wellman

Ferne Press

King of Dilly Dally
Copyright © 2009 by Michael D. Scott
Illustrations by Megan D. Wellman
Creative Designs by Jill Chambers

Printed in Canada

The Acknowledgment page contains lyrics from "*Private Suit*" by Bettie Serveert, copyright 2000, reprinted with the permission of Sony/ATV Music Publishing.

Summary: The concept of this story is truth, discovery, understanding, communication, and growth, which explain how balance is the key to a happy, progressive life.

Library of Congress Cataloging-in-Publication Data
Scott, Michael D.
King of Dilly Dally/Michael D. Scott – First Edition
ISBN-13: 978-1-933916-35-4
1. Juvenile fiction. 2. Self-help. 3. Childhood. 4. Upper Elementary. 5. Middle school.
I. Scott, Michael D. II. King of Dilly Dally
Library of Congress Control Number: 2008944185

Illustrations were created using water colors and acrylic pencils.

FERNE PRESS

Ferne Press is an imprint of Nelson Publishing & Marketing
366 Welch Road, Northville, MI 48167
www.nelsonpublishingandmarketing.com
(248) 735-0418

Dedication

I dedicate this book to my son, Kyle. You are my inspiration for all that I do, and you have impacted my life in ways that I could have never imagined.

Acknowledgments

Thank you to Kyle, Melissa, Jay, Parker, Ruby, Duffy, Riki, Joe, Ryan, Hal Scott and the entire Scott Family, Megan D. Wellman, Nicola Rooney, Bethany Gatto, Sherry Suggs, Igor, Irina, Timor, Vera, Jasmine Wang, Darl and Marcia Williams, Ian, Laura, Greg, Ted and Marlene Geheb, Linda, Laura, Rachel, Michele Taipalus, Kimberly Hopper, Alicia Lundell, Anna Stanaway, Nick, Nic, and Nikki, Loftradamus, Keith and Kate Dombrowski, Ken Sills, Matt Ciantar, Carol Hartford, Ron and Jeff Archambault, David Resseguie, Steve and Tammy Watson, Carol van Dyk, Peter Visser, Hermann Bunskoeke, Reiner Veldman, Tom Johnston, Lacey Chemsak, Curtis LeRoy Foreman, Mike Fisk, Dave "Guten" Morgan, and for her kindness and advice, Carol McCloud.

Lastly, thank you to Marian Nelson, Kris Yankee, Kawita Kandpal, and all at Nelson Publishing for their hard work, guidance, educational vision, and collaborative nature.

Hey, don't worry about me,
I'll be sitting by the seashore,
Laughing at the life forms,
And whistling down the breeze.
So don't worry about me,
Because you can't please everyone,
And I'm thinking to myself,
And I'm not the only one,
We all gotta learn
To give some in return,
Like little works of wonder.

from "Private Suit" by Bettie Serveert
Copyright 2000

Hal's 1955 Chevy

In loving memory of my uncle, Hal Scott, 1948 – 2008.

Introduction

This story was written for children of all ages to have a better understanding of the importance of discovery, communication, and balance. Children can read the story of King Bill and comprehend that it is ultimately their decision as individuals to make good choices and learn how to maintain a balance in all they do in life.

Children have an enormous capacity for learning, and when we, as adults, use a wider range of words and concepts when speaking with them, they will undoubtedly begin to put them to use. Consequently, this offers our children a chance to build character for themselves, respect for others, and love for the world in which they live.

–Michael D. Scott

"The final forming of a person's character lies in their own hands."

-Anne Frank

In the region of Dilly Dally,
there lives a boy who is king,
and his name is Bill Dally—
that's him there on the swing.

Dilly Dally is a region
in the nation of Procrasta,
where what should be done today
is often done afta.

And if you look and look closely,
then you'll see the relation,
of why the people of Procrasta,
call it the Procrasta Nation.

For King Bill has a saying,
and if it's attention you're paying,
you'll often hear him chime,
"No I won't, so I won't!
For I don't have the time.
To waste my whole day working
when 'fun' is somewhere lurking,
would surely be a crime."

"But King Bill here's a bill
that you have to sign."
"No I won't, so I won't!
For I don't have the time."

"But King Bill there are people,
and it's money they need borrow."
But the people knew very well,
and it filled their hearts with sorrow.
King Bill's favorite word is "won't,"
and it's King Bill they must follow.
"No I won't, so I won't!
Perhaps I'll get to it tomorrow."

"But King Bill hear our plea,
who will get these things done?
Our neighboring Nation of Aboma,
or the Aboma Nation,
have stated they'd like to make
these two great Nations one."
"No I won't, so I won't!
I'd rather bask in the sun."

"I'd rather sit here by our lake,
a lake so big it's like an ocean.
To frolic in the fields,
and observe all things in motion—
the butterflies, the trees, the breeze—
and if I had the notion,
I would share what I have learned,
and put it in a potion."

"Although there's much work to do,
I would rather have fun.
No I won't, so I won't!
And the deal is done."

"If you won't, then you won't,"
so said his Mum with concern.
"But if you daydream all day,
tell me what will you learn?
And if you don't, then you don't,
but tell me what you foresee—
if not the 'King of Dilly Dally,'
then what and where will you be?"

King Bill smiled at his Mum and replied softly,
"Each night as I lie alone I do question.
I think about Procrasta,
and the things you have mentioned,
and what stands out in my mind
is the ever-growing elation,
of what I love about Dilly Dally,
and the Procrasta Nation."

"For I've seen the beauty of dawn,
where the earth meets the rising sun,
not seeing them as two,
rather the two of them as one.
I have watched a green leaf
as it shakes morning dew,
with the warmth of the sun
as the day starts anew."

"Or the coolness of the lake
as it cleanses my skin,
and a fish swims by
with the flip of its fin.
To lie in the sand
as the wind gently sings,
I am safe and warm
with thoughts of beautiful things."

"I have often thought
to show you these sights,
and stargaze with you
under soft moonlight.
A moon not too bright,
shining brilliant, no less,
just the right shade of pale,
is our stargazing guest."

"To spot satellites
as they're cruising the sky,
so nimble, so swift,
clandestine, and sly."

"To witness the wonders
of this world indeed,
I daydream and learn
and my heart concedes
that the simple yet wonderful
things that are true,
are what matter most to me, Mum,
if that gives you a clue."

King Bill's Mum understood
and had something to say,
"You have learned many things
from what you observe each day.
And I'm so proud of you Bill
that you think this way.
But there's a little more to life,
and a man you'll someday be.
So it's never too early
to live responsibly."

"For there truly is a balance,
and it's up to you to find—
to care for Dilly Dally,
and then to find the time,
to enjoy what you love,
and to be of sound mind.
And if you attain this balance,
it will be your gain, and mine.
Then the Kingdom of Dilly Dally
will have a king who is kind."

"A king who is kind,
and one who understands
that there are chores to be done
for this beautiful land.
And you can set the example,
for it's all in your hands,
and the nation of Procrasta
will be a nation that stands."

King Bill understood
his Mum's words and her plight,
for Bill was listening all along
much to his Mum's delight.
"Now why don't we call it good,
and for now say goodnight.
Sleep well my Boy King,
I'll see you at first light."

And as Bill fell asleep
with his mind full of wonder,
his Mum's words echoed clear
and those words he did ponder.
"To not find a balance
would truly be a blunder.
But to care for Dilly Dally,
my heart will grow fonder."

In the morn' King Bill awoke,
filled with a new sensation.
For he had something to share
with the Procrasta Nation.

People gathered from near and far
to hear King Bill's proclamation,
with open ears, attentively,
and with great anticipation.

"To my people of Procrasta,
I have something to say.
No longer will I put off
what should be done today.
I'll be a responsible king
and balance work and play.
To live, love, and learn,
and have fun along the way."

"So…

I hereby accept my throne,
I now call it my own.
It is time that I get my fill.
My first act as king
is to shake this 'won't' thing,
I am changing my name to 'Will!'"

FIN

Glossary

Words are listed as they appear in the text.

region: a broad geographic area distinguished by similar features.

lurking: concealed but capable of being discovered; lying hidden.

bill: a written document or note; a formal petition.

plea: a humble request for help from someone in authority.

frolic: to amuse oneself; make merry.

observe: to watch carefully, especially with attention to details or behavior.

notion: a general concept; a personal inclination.

potion: a mixture of liquids (as medicine).

foresee: to see (as a development) beforehand.

clandestine: marked by, held in, or conducted with secrecy.

concedes: accepts as true, valid, or accurate.

attain: to reach as an end.

plight: an unfortunate, difficult, or precarious situation.

echoed: repeated, imitated; restated in support or agreement.

ponder: to weigh in the mind; to think about or reflect on.

blunder: an error or mistake resulting usually from stupidity, ignorance, or carelessness.

fonder: more affectionate or loving.

sensation: a state of excited interest or feeling.

attentively: in a mindful or observant manner.

anticipation: the act of looking forward; a pleasurable expectation.

proclamation: an official formal public announcement.

All definitions are taken from *Webster's Dictionary* and *Webster's Online Dictionary*.

About the Author

Michael D. Scott lives in Michigan. His love of writing, music, and nature prompted him to write *King of Dilly Dally*. He greatly enjoys the outdoors and spends much of his time writing, camping, kayaking, and playing tennis and ice hockey.

About the Illustrator

Megan D. Wellman grew up in Redford, Michigan and currently resides with her husband, two Great Danes, and a cat in Canton, Michigan. She holds a bachelor's degree in fine arts from Eastern Michigan University with a minor in children's theater.

King of Dilly Dally is Megan's sixth book. Her books include *This Babe So Small, Lonely Teddy, Grandma's Ready, . . . and that is why we teach,* and *Being Bella*, which are all available from Ferne Press.